GIRL vs ROCK!

Diary Disaster

Holly Smith Dinbergs

illustrated by
Chantal Stewart

D1143906

RISING STARS

First published in Great Britain by
RISING STARS UK LTD 2005
76 Farnaby Road, Bromley, BR1 4BH

Reprinted 2006 (twice)

For information visit our website at:
www.risingstars-uk.com

British Library Cataloguing in Publication Data

A CIP record for this book is available from the British Library.

ISBN: 1-905056-22-2

First published in 2005 by
MACMILLAN EDUCATION AUSTRALIA PTY LTD
627 Chapel Street, South Yarra, Australia 3141

Visit our website at www.macmillan.com.au

Associated companies and representatives throughout the world.

Series created by Felice Arena and Phil Kettle
Project Management by Limelight Press Pty Ltd
Cover and text design by Lore Foye
Illustrations by Chantal Stewart

Printed and bound in Great Britain by
Mackays of Chatham plc, Chatham, Kent

GIRLS ROCK!
Contents

Sophie   Jess

I've Got a Problem!

The phone rings at Jess's house. She grabs it with one hand while she holds an ice-cream cornet in the other. It's her best friend, Sophie.

Jess "Hello?"

Sophie (upset) "Jess. It's me. Can you come over?"

Jess "When?"

Sophie "Now. Right now!"

Jess (worried) "What's the matter? What's happened?"

Sophie "Well, someone's been reading my diary!"

Jess "No way. You don't even let *me* read your diary!"

Sophie "Exactly. That's because a diary's private. It's where you write really personal things that no-one else is supposed to read."

Jess "You mean things about you and Josh? You like him, I know."

Sophie "I don't like Josh."

Jess "Yes, you do!"

Sophie "Look, I don't. But forget that for now! Please will you come over and help me?"

Jess "OK, but wait while I ask."

Jess moves the phone away from her mouth and asks her mum if she can go to Sophie's.

Jess "Mum says it's okay as long as I'm back for dinner."

Sophie "Cool, then hurry."
Jess "I'll be right over."

Jess hangs up the phone. She puts on her jacket and races out of the front door. Her ice-cream drips as she runs along.

CHAPTER 2

Diary Detectives

A few minutes later, Sophie hears the doorbell ring. She opens the door to find Jess standing there.

Sophie "Were you eating chocolate?"
Jess "How did you know?"
Sophie "Because you've got
  chocolate all over your face."

Blushing, Jess wipes her mouth.

Sophie "Come upstairs. You've got to see this."

The girls head for Sophie's bedroom. On the way they pass Puffles, Sophie's new cat.

Jess "So *this* is Puffles! Is it a him or a her?"

Sophie "A him."

Jess "He's so cute! I wish I could have a cat but my dad says he can't take any more animals in the house."

Sophie "That's because you already have a dog, three goldfish, two hermit crabs and a budgie. I don't think a cat could fit!"

The girls go into Sophie's room and close the door. Jess sits on the bed while Sophie paces up and down the room.

Jess "So what's happened?"
Sophie "You know how I always write in my diary every night before I go to sleep."
Jess "Mmmm ... "

Sophie "Then I hide it under the bed."

Jess "Come on ... spit it out!"

Sophie "Well, this morning when I came back from dance class, I found it over there!"

Sophie points at a small, red book on the floor. Clipped to the lock strap on the book is a small, green, stuffed turtle.

Jess "Hey, that's the diary I gave you for Christmas. Where did you get the turtle?"

Sophie "In my Christmas stocking."

Jess "It looks really cool."

The girls stare at the diary for a few seconds, both looking very serious.

Jess "Sophie, nobody can read your diary. It's got a lock on it."

Sophie "Yes, but it doesn't lock because I lost the key. It just looks locked."

Jess "Oh. Hmm ... who do you think did it?"

Sophie "Well ... I wrote in my diary last night as usual and put it under the bed. So it must have happened this morning."

Jess "What about your family? Could one of them have done it?"

Sophie "My dad left early to play golf, plus he never comes into my room. Mum went shopping and my sister slept over at her friend's. That just leaves my brother. He's always doing stupid things just to annoy me."

Jess (nodding) "This sounds like
   something your brother would do.
   So what are you going to do about
   it?"

Sophie "Set a trap, and catch him
   red-handed!"

Jess sits straight up.

CHAPTER 3

Setting the Trap

Jess looks at Sophie and chuckles.
She likes the sound of a trap.

Jess "A trap? Cool!"

Sophie "Yes, we've got to catch him."

Jess "So what are you going to do
to him if we catch him?"

Sophie "I don't know. Something
really horrible. He'll be sorry."

The girls see Sophie's brother race past her door. Next they hear his bedroom door slam shut.

Sophie "Here's the plan. I'll put the diary back under my bed. Then we'll pretend to leave."

Jess "What do you mean 'pretend to leave'?"

Sophie (whispering) "Well, we'll make it sound like we're leaving but we'll really just hide in the wardrobe. Once he thinks I'm gone, I bet a million pounds he comes back and tries to read more. Then I'll get him!"

Jess "OK. So how do we pretend we're leaving?"

Sophie "Easy. Just do what I do."

Sophie beckons to Jess, who follows her down the hallway until they are standing in front of her brother's door.

Sophie (shouting) "Come on, Jess. Let's go *outside*. Are you ready to go *outside*?"
Jess (shouting back) "Yes. I'm ready to go *outside*."

Sophie (still shouting) "OK, OK, let's get going."

The girls walk to the front door. Sophie opens it, then slams it shut. The loud noise makes the girls jump. They start to giggle as they tiptoe back to Sophie's room. Sophie shoves her diary back under the bed.

Sophie "Come on, get in the wardrobe."

The girls walk into the wardrobe, pushing Sophie's shoes to one side to make room to sit on the floor.

Sophie "I'd forgotten how many shoes are in here. They're everywhere!"

Jess "I suppose they are! So now we just wait."

CHAPTER 4

Waiting for Results

The girls are sitting in the wardrobe, waiting for some movement outside.

Jess "Do you have anything to eat?"

Sophie "You're joking. We're in the wardrobe, not the kitchen."

Jess "I know, but I thought maybe you had stuff in here."

A few minutes later, Jess changes
position.

Jess "I wish *somebody* would hurry
up and come. My legs are getting
cramp. And I'm thirsty. Anything
to drink in here?"

Sophie "No of course not."

Jess "I'm going to lie down. Looks like we could be here for a while."

Sophie "OK, but watch your feet on my clothes."

Jess "It's really comfortable down here. You should try it."

Sophie "Jess, keep still or he'll hear us."

Jess "OK, OK. When do you think he's going to come?"

Sophie "Shhh. We're supposed to be quiet. He might hear us."

Jess (whispering loudly) "This is boring."

Sophie "Do you want to play a game?

Jess "OK. What game? Where's your Gameboy?"

Sophie "It's on my desk."

Jess "Can you get it?"

Sophie "Well … I could. But if he walks by just as I'm getting out of the wardrobe, our plan will be ruined."

Jess "Hey, I know what we can play, Truth or Dare."

Sophie "Truth or Dare? No, I'll get the Gameboy."

Jess "You never like playing Truth or Dare because you're afraid I'll ask you an embarrassing question—like 'Do you like Josh?'."

Sophie "Umm... I have to go to the bathroom. You stay here. I'll go and get some yummy biscuits from the kitchen too—chocolate OK?"

Jess "Now you're talking!"

Sophie crawls slowly out of the wardrobe and tiptoes to her door. She leaves the room, pulling the door behind her so that it's open just a little bit.

Jess (to herself) "I'm bored in here. Hey, there's the Gameboy!"

Jess decides to get out of the wardrobe and gets the Gameboy off the desk. Just as she's about to make her move, the bedroom door swings slowly open. Her mouth drops as she watches what happens.

Jess "Hey Sophie, I caught him!"

CHAPTER 5

Surprise!

Sophie bursts through the door,
looking really angry.

Sophie "You creep! How dare you
read my diary!"

Jess "Sophie, you shouldn't talk to
Puffles that way."

Sophie "Huh?"

Jess is sitting on the floor stroking Puffles. The diary is next to them.

Sophie "Where's my creep of a brother?"

Jess (laughing) "Not here. Just me and Puffles."

Sophie "How did my diary get there?"

Jess "Just watch this."

Sophie "What?"

Jess "Move the diary a bit. You know, just give it a push."

Sophie flicks the diary away from her. Puffles chases after it.

Sophie "Puffles, don't play with my diary. Leave it here!"

Sophie starts to laugh.

Sophie "Oh, no! So it wasn't my brother after all."

Jess "No. It was innocent little Puffles. So nobody's read your diary, unless it's in catspeak!"

Jess picks up the diary.

Jess "I bet if I read this it would say, 'I love Josh'."

Sophie snatches the diary out of
Jess's hands and shoves it into her
desk drawer.

Sophie "It does not! This diary is
off-limits to everyone and that
includes best friends and
especially nosey cats!"

GIRLS ROCK!
Diary Lingo

Jess

Sophie

code Special signs or messages that you use to write in your diary, to stop someone else (like an annoying brother) reading it.

diary It's where you write really private things—almost every day—about what you're doing, what you're thinking or feeling.

journal Another word for a diary.

memoir A book you can write when you're older that talks about things you did, thought and felt at different points in your life—it's not done day by day.

secrets Things you write in your diary that absolutely no-one else can know.

GIRLS ROCK!

Diary Must-dos

☆ If you get a diary, get one with a lock so no-one can sneak a look at what you write.

☆ Don't lose the key!

☆ Write every day at the same time, so you get into the diary-writing habit.

☆ Write the date each time you write in your diary.

☆ Don't confuse the word "diary" with "dairy"—if you say you're going to write in your "dairy", people will think you're off to see the cows!

☆ Write down your dreams in your diary—some people say that dreams are the key to what you really think!

☆ Write in your diary with a special pen (maybe with a cool colour) because it's just more fun.

☆ Write in code if you're worried about somebody reading your diary.

☆ Keep your diary secret! If you think someone else might read it, you might not be really honest, and diaries are supposed to contain the truth.

GIRLS ROCK!

Diary Instant Info

The best-selling diary of all time is "The Diary of Anne Frank". It has sold over 25 million copies and has been translated into 55 languages. Anne's diary tells the true story of her life from age 12 to 14 when she and her family were living secretly in an attic during World War II.

A ship's captain keeps a diary for the ship. It's called the ship's "log".

Bridget Jones's Diary was a book first, and then a movie—but Bridget is not a real person and it's not a real diary. It's a story told in the form of a diary.

There are websites designed to help people write diaries online. But most people like to use special books that they can take everywhere.

Famous people (like politicians) often keep diaries so that they have a record of special events. They keep this record in case they want to sell their thoughts, or memoirs, one day for thousands of pounds.

GIRLS ROCK!
Think Tank

1 Can anyone write a diary?

2 What kind of diary is best?

3 What kind of pen should you use to write in your diary?

4 Who wrote the best-selling diary of all time?

5 Where should you hide your diary?

6 Where can you buy a diary?

7 Do all diaries have locks?

8 Secrets are written in diaries. True or false?

Answers

1 Anybody can write a diary. Just get a book, note the date and start writing!

2 The best kind of diary is one with a lock.

3 Ideally, you should use one with disappearing ink to write in your diary—that way, nobody can read what you write, including you!

4 Anne Frank, who received a diary for her twelfth birthday, wrote the best-selling diary of all time.

5 You should hide your diary somewhere your cat (or brother) can't find it.

6 You can buy diaries in shops that sell pens and paper such as newsagents and stationery shops.

7 Not all diaries have locks.

8 It's true. People love to write down their secrets in diaries.

How did you score?

- If you got 8 answers correct, you're ready to write a book called *Everything You Ever Wanted to Know About Diaries* or just have your own diary.

- If you got 6 answers correct, you might ask for a new diary for your next birthday.

- If you got 4 answers correct, try not to confuse "diary" with "dairy"!

39

Hey Girls!

I love to read and hope you do, too. The first book I really loved was a book called "Mary Poppins". It was full of magic (well before Harry Potter) and I got hooked on reading. I went to the library every Saturday and left with a pile of books so heavy I could hardly carry them!

Here are some ideas about how you can make "Diary Disaster" even more fun. At school, you and your friends can be actors and put on this story as a play. To bring the story to life, bring in some props from home such as a small red book and a stuffed cat. Maybe you could create a bedroom too.

Who will be Jess? Who will be Sophie? Who will be the narrator? (That's the person who reads the parts between when Jess or Sophie say something.) Once you've decided on these details, you're ready to act out the story in front of the class. I bet everyone will clap when you are finished. Hey, a talent scout from a television station might just be watching!

See if somebody at home will read this story out loud with you. Reading at home is important and a lot of fun as well.

Do you know what my dad used to tell me? "Readers are leaders".

And, remember, Girls Rock!

Holly Smith Dinbergs

GIRLS ROCK!
When We Were Kids

Holly

Julie

Holly talked to Julie, another *Girls Rock!* author.

Holly "Did you have a diary when you were young?"

Julie "Of course I did!"

Holly "Did anyone ever read it?"

Julie "Just a boy on a bus."

Holly "Really? How did you know it was him?"

Julie "He called me to say he'd found the diary on a bus."

Holly "Did you get it back unopened?"

Julie "He said he hadn't opened it. But the bits of melted chocolate on the pages gave him away."

GIRLS ROCK!
What a Laugh!

Q What do cats like to read?

A "Mews" papers.

GIRLS ROCK!

Read about the fun
that girls have in these
GIRLS ROCK! titles:

The Sleepover

Pool Pals

Bowling Buddies

Girl Pirates

Netball Showdown

School Play Stars

Diary Disaster

Horsing Around

GIRLS ROCK! books are available from
most booksellers. For mail order information
please call Rising Stars on 01933 443862 or visit
www.risingstars-uk.com